REMARKABLE PEOPLE

Taylor Swift

by

Anita Yasuda

BOOK CODE

T15143

AV² by Weigl brings you media enhanced books that support active learning.

AV² provides enriched content that supplements and complements this book. Weigl's AV² books strive to create inspired learning and engage young minds for a total learning experience.

Go to www.av2books.com, and enter this book's unique code. You will have access to video, audio, web links, quizzes, a slide show, and activities.

Audio
Listen to sections of the book read aloud.

Video
Watch informative video clips.

Web Link
Find research sites and play interactive games.

Try This!
Complete activities and hands-on experiments.

Due to the dynamic nature of the Internet, some of the URLs and activities provided as part of AV² by Weigl may have changed or ceased to exist. AV² by Weigl accepts no responsibility for any such changes. All media enhanced books are regularly monitored to update addresses and sites in a timely manner. Contact AV² by Weigl at 1-866-649-3445 or av2books@weigl.com with any questions, comments, or feedback.

Published by AV² by Weigl
350 5th Avenue, 59th Floor
New York, NY 10118

www.av2books.com   www.weigl.com

Copyrihgt ©2011 AV² by Weigl

All rights reserved. No part of this publication may be reproduced, stored in a retrieval system, or transmitted in any form or by any means, electronic, mechanical, photocopying, recording, or otherwise, without the prior written permission of the publisher.

Library of Congress Cataloging-in-Publication Data

Yasuda, Anita.
  Taylor Swift / Anita Yasuda.
      p. cm. -- (Remarkable people)
  Includes index.
  ISBN 978-1-61690-157-8 (hardcover : alk. paper) -- ISBN 978-1-61690-158-5 (softcover : alk. paper) -- ISBN 978-1-61690-159-2 (e-book)
 1. Swift, Taylor, 1989--Juvenile literature. 2. Singers--United States--Biography--Juvenile literature. 3. Women country musicians--United States--Biography--Juvenile literature. I. Title.
  ML3930.S989Y37 2011
  782.421642092--dc22
      [B]
                                       2010006163

Printed in the United States of America in North Mankato, Minnesota
1 2 3 4 5 6 7 8 9 0   14 13 12 11 10

052010
WEP264000

Editor: Heather Kissock
Design: Terry Paulhus

Photograph Credits
Weigl acknowledges Getty Images as the primary image supplier for this title.

Every reasonable effort has been made to trace ownership and to obtain permission to reprint copyright material. The publishers would be pleased to have any errors or omissions brought to their attention so that they may be corrected in subsequent printings.

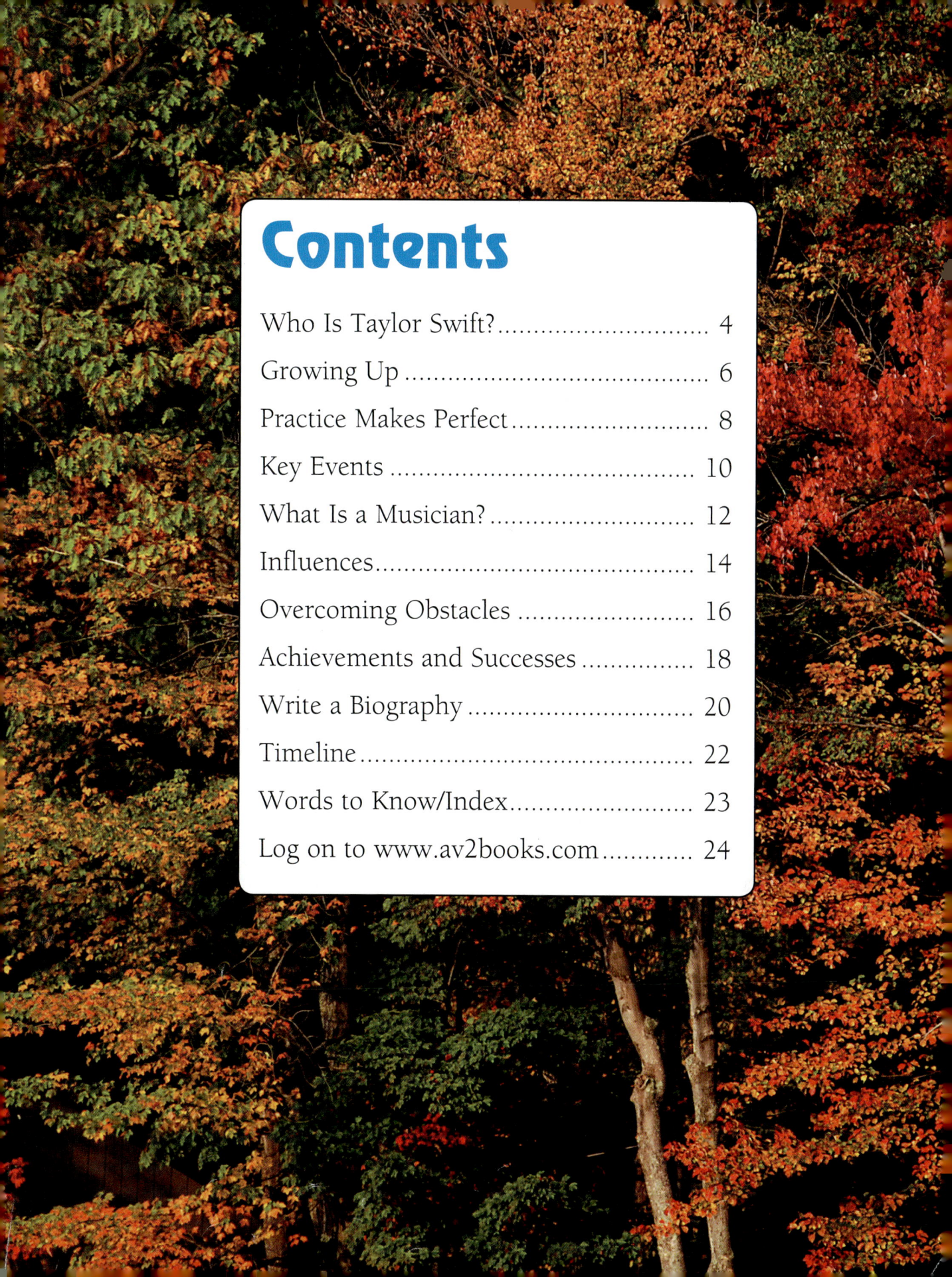

Contents

Who Is Taylor Swift?............................ 4
Growing Up 6
Practice Makes Perfect........................ 8
Key Events 10
What Is a Musician?............................ 12
Influences.. 14
Overcoming Obstacles 16
Achievements and Successes 18
Write a Biography 20
Timeline 22
Words to Know/Index........................ 23
Log on to www.av2books.com 24

Who Is Taylor Swift?

Taylor Swift is one of the brightest stars in country music. This talented performer released her first album in 2006. The **album** produced five consecutive top 10 **singles**, which was a new record for a female, solo artist. Her single, "Our Song," went all the way to number one. This was only the beginning of Taylor's success.

Two years later, in 2008, Taylor's second album, Fearless, was released. It held the top spot on the **Billboard** chart for 11 weeks. Later that year, she was named Entertainer of the Year at the Country Music Awards. This made Taylor the youngest artist in history to win the award.

"What I've learned is not to change who you are, because eventually you're going to run out of new things to become."

Taylor's friendly and outgoing image has earned her fans around the world. She is known to stay hours after shows until she has signed autographs for her fans. When she is not performing, Taylor uses her fame to raise money for homeless animals, underprivileged children, and other charities.

Growing Up

Taylor Alison Swift was born on December 13, 1989, in Reading, Pennsylvania. She grew up on a Christmas tree farm in the town of Wyomissing. Her mother, Andrea, stayed at home to care for Taylor and her younger brother, Austin. Her father, Scott, was a **stockbroker**. As a child, Taylor rode horses **competitively**, but her main hobby was singing.

When she was 10 years old, Taylor began singing locally. She sang at karaoke contests, coffee houses, fairs, and festivals. Taylor was focused on becoming a musician.

■ Taylor's love of words was apparent at an early age. In fourth grade, she won a national poetry contest for a poem titled "Monster in My Closet."

Get to Know Pennsylvania

MAMMAL
White-Tailed Deer

TREE
Eastern Hemlock

FLOWER
Mountain Laurel

Harrisburg is the capital of Pennsylvania. Philadelphia is the state's largest city.

The first reading of the Declaration of Independence was at Philadelphia's Independence Square on July 8, 1776.

In 1775, Johann Behrent built the first piano in America in Philadelphia. He called it the "Piano Forte."

The state nickname is the Keystone State.

The Liberty Bell is one of Philadelphia's biggest tourist attractions. It was rung to signal the first reading of the Declaration of Independence.

From a young age, Taylor Swift knew that she wanted to be a performer. In order to achieve her goal, Taylor wrote her own songs and taught herself to play guitar. Have you ever had to learn a new skill in order to accomplish a goal? What was the hardest part about learning this new skill? In what ways can you put this skill to use?

Remarkable People

Practice Makes Perfect

Taylor always knew she wanted to be a singer and began working toward her goals at a young age. In her hometown, Taylor was a regular participant in the weekly karaoke contest at the Pat Garrett Roadhouse. The prize for winning the contest was to open for country stars such as the Charlie Daniels Band and George Jones. Taylor sang every week for a year and a half until she won.

Her parents were impressed by her hard work. When she was 11, they began taking regular trips to Nashville. There, she performed and met with songwriters in the area. That same year, Taylor was invited to sing "The Star-Spangled Banner" before a Philadelphia 76ers basketball game. Rapper Jay-Z was in the audience at the game. At the end of her performance, he gave her a high-five. She was thrilled.

When she was 12, Taylor learned how to play the guitar. A friend taught her three **chords**. Taylor then went on to teach herself how to play more difficult chords. She began using the guitar to help her write songs.

■ When Taylor was teaching herself to play guitar, she practiced until her fingers hurt.

Taylor Swift

When Taylor was 13, her family moved to Nashville. Taylor tried to break into the music business by dropping off **demos** at record companies. At 14, she landed a job as a songwriter working for Sony/ATV Publishing. At the same time, Taylor was experiencing her first year of high school. Even though she was an A student, Taylor decided to be homeschooled so that she could focus on her music career.

> **QUICK FACTS**
> - Taylor's **debut** album sold more than three million copies.
> - Taylor ran a charity auction to help homeless animals in Puerto Rico.
> - Taylor's favorite color is white.

One evening, while performing at the Bluebird Café in Nashville, Taylor caught the attention of Scott Borchetta, a music industry executive. He signed her to his new **record label**, Big Machine Records. Taylor recorded her album over a four-month period. She had written or co-written all of the songs on the album. The album, called Taylor Swift, was released in 2006.

■ Experienced songwriter Liz Rose co-wrote the Grammy-award-winning song "White Horse" with Taylor.

Remarkable People

Key Events

Taylor's album was an instant success. It quickly earned **double platinum** status. On Billboard's Hot Country Songs chart, three songs from the album, "Tim McGraw," "Teardrops on My Guitar," and "Our Song," became top 10 singles.

Taylor began doing radio station tours to promote her songs. Most tours last six weeks, but Taylor's lasted six months. She wanted to meet every person who had helped her achieve success. Following her radio station tour, she went on tour as the opening act for the country music group Rascal Flatts.

Taylor's second album, Fearless, was released in 2008. It debuted at number one on Billboard's top 200 chart. This album went six times platinum, selling more than 6 million copies. In 2009, Taylor toured North America as a **headline act**. She ended the year by being named the Associated Press Association's Entertainer of the Year.

■ At the 51st Grammy Awards, Taylor performed with fellow teen sensation Miley Cyrus. They sang Taylor's hit "Fifteen."

Thoughts from Taylor

Taylor works hard to succeed in her career and life. Here are some of her thoughts about touring, music, and life.

Taylor talks about why she does not "Google" herself.
"It's very tempting. But if you read something about yourself it makes you wonder what the public perception is of you."

Taylor talks about when she writes music.
"I write when I'm frustrated, angry, or confused. I've figured out a way to filter all of that into something good."

Taylor talks about touring
"I've had to adjust. You can't be particular about where you write songs, you can't be particular about where you feel comfortable—home becomes anywhere with a bed."

Taylor talks about her music career.
"For me it was never about being famous because my ultimate dream was for people to care about the words that I wrote."

Taylor talks about the importance of education.
"Education has always been at the forefront of my priorities, so I'm really glad to have my diploma."

Taylor talks about her relationship with her brother.
"We used to fight like cats and dogs but when I went on the road I started really missing him."

Remarkable People 11

What Is a Musician?

A musician is a person who can play an instrument, sing, or write music. Some musicians, such as Taylor Swift, have all three skills. A musician can work alone as a solo artist or may perform with a group.

Creating music is challenging. It takes a great deal of work. Professional musicians spend hours practicing and rehearsing. They work hard to write songs that express their feelings and can entertain their fans. Performances are often at night and on weekends. Some musicians tour from place to place. They may travel around the world to perform.

When performing, musicians often develop their own distinctive style. This may mean dressing a certain way or having a unique sound.

■ Taylor's songs are often about events or situations that she has experienced.

Taylor Swift

Musicians 101

Miley Cyrus (1992–)

Miley is an actor, singer, and songwriter. She was born in Franklin, Tennessee. Her father is actor and country singer Billy Ray Cyrus. Miley **auditioned** for the television show *Hannah Montana* when she was 11 years old but was turned down. She kept trying to get the attention of the **producers** by sending them videotapes of herself performing. A year later, she was given the role. Miley made music history in 2007, when she became the youngest artist in the United States to have two, number one hit albums in less than one year.

Nick Jonas (1992–)

Nick is one-third of the musical group Jonas Brothers. He is a singer, songwriter, and actor. Nick was born in Dallas, Texas. He began singing as soon as he could talk. Nick made his Broadway debut at the age of seven. He appeared in many professional musicals including *Les Miserables* and *The Sound of Music*. His film debut followed in 2008 with the Disney Channel Original Movie called *Camp Rock*.

Justin Bieber (1994–)

Justin is a self-taught musician. He can play the guitar, drums, piano, and trumpet. Justin was born in Stratford, Ontario, Canada. By the age of 15, he was a YouTube sensation. Videos of him performing **cover versions** of songs were viewed more than 10 million times. Singer Usher was so impressed by the videos that he flew Justin to Atlanta, Georgia, for a meeting. Justin was then signed to Island Def Jam record label. He released his debut album *My World* in 2009.

Selena Gomez (1992–)

Selena is a musician and actor. She was born in Grand Prairie, Texas. She is best known for her role as Alex Russo on the Disney Channel Original Series *Wizards of Waverly Place*. In 2008, Selena signed a deal with Hollywood Records. She sang on the *Tinker Bell*, *Another Cinderella Story*, and *Wizards of Waverly Place* soundtracks. In 2009, she released her debut album *Kiss & Tell*. Selena has been **nominated** for and won several awards, including 2009's Teen Choice Award for Choice Red Carpet Icon and Choice Summer TV Star.

Guitars

Many musicians play the guitar. An acoustic guitar makes sound when the player plucks one of the guitar's six strings. The vibrations move inside the hollow guitar and become louder. An electric guitar sends vibrations to an **amplifier** and speaker.

Influences

Taylor's parents have had a strong influence on her. From a young age, they recognized Taylor's talent and supported her dreams. They moved to Hendersonville, a suburb of Nashville, so their daughter could live closer to the center of the country music industry. Since her success, Taylor's parents have traveled on tours with her. This support has kept Taylor focused.

Another influence in Taylor's life was her grandmother, Angela Ann. Angela was a professional opera singer who was successful in many parts of the world. Every Sunday, Taylor listened to her grandmother sing in church.

Taylor has always enjoyed country music. When she was young, she loved Patsy Cline and Dolly Parton. She also listened to LeAnn Rimes and Tina Turner. Taylor admired the Dixie Chicks because they played their own instruments and experimented musically.

■ Like Taylor, LeAnn Rimes was a country music sensation in her teens. LeAnn had won two Grammys before she turned 14.

Country music superstar Shania Twain also influenced Taylor. Taylor said that Shania did a great job of making herself memorable. Shania did this by writing catchy songs. Taylor has tried to do the same.

Taylor noticed that, when Shania toured, her shows were big productions with great **choreography**, **sets**, and costumes. Taylor included these elements in her first headlining tour. Her set for the Fearless tour included several costume changes and a fairy tale castle.

THE SWIFT FAMILY

Taylor may have sold millions of records and toured the world, but her home is still in Tennessee. Until 2009, Taylor lived with her mother, Andrea, her father, Scott, and her brother, Austin. Then, she purchased her first home in downtown Nashville, Tennessee. She now lives in a penthouse condo with her dog, Bug, a mini pinscher. Taylor also has a cat named Indi.

■ Taylor begged her parents to take her to Nashville. She had seen a television special on Shania Twain and Faith Hill. It said they went to Nashville to succeed in the music industry.

Remarkable People

Overcoming Obstacles

From a young age, Taylor knew that she wanted to be a musician. While other children were playing soccer or attending parties, Taylor was writing songs and learning to play the guitar.

When Taylor was in middle school, she felt like she did not fit in with her schoolmates. She coped with this negative experience by writing songs about her feelings.

When she was 11 years old, Taylor made her first trip to Nashville, where she hoped to get a record deal. She walked into the offices of every record label in Nashville and gave them her demo tape. While waiting for her career to start, Taylor continued writing songs and performing. She wanted to bring attention to her talent.

■ Taylor's mother continues to support her daughter's career. The two often attend awards ceremonies together.

At age 13, Taylor's hard work paid off. A record company called RCA offered her a recording **contract**. Taylor accepted their offer. However, when they would not allow her to record her own songs, she decided to leave the company the next year. Around this time, her songwriting skills were recognized by Sony/ATV. She became the youngest staff songwriter the company had ever hired. Taylor kept performing and, eventually, was signed by the label Big Machine Records. Success soon followed.

■ Taylor wrote the song "Tim McGraw" while preparing for her first album. It is based on a song Tim wrote called "Can't Tell Me Nothin'."

Achievements and Successes

Taylor has already been given some of the music industry's top awards. On the strength of her first album alone, she won the Country Music Association's Horizon Award. This award is given to a new country artist who has shown the most growth in the industry. In 2008, the Academy of Country Music awarded Taylor its Top New Female Artist award.

In 2009, Taylor had eight songs on the Billboard Hot 100 chart at the same time. This success won Fearless the Album of the Year award at both the Academy of Country Music Awards and the Country Music Association Awards. Taylor became the youngest person in history to win the Country Music Association's Entertainer of the Year award. She was the year's top winner, with four awards in total.

■ Taylor was the first solo female to win Entertainer of the Year in a decade. Taylor's idol, Shania Twain, had won in 1999.

That same year, Taylor then went on to win five American Music awards. The awards included Artist of the Year and Favorite Country Album. In September 2009, she became the first country music artist to win an MTV Video Music Award (VMA). She won the Best Female Video VMA for her single "You Belong With Me."

Taylor has also branched out into other areas of entertainment, including acting. One of her career highlights was hosting and performing in skits on the comedy show *Saturday Night Live*. Taylor also had a role in a motion picture called *Valentine's Day*.

HELPING OTHERS

Often, musicians use their popularity to increase public awareness. They may bring attention to nonprofit organizations, environmental issues, or help fund special causes. Taylor lends her support to many charitable organizations. In December 2009, Taylor donated her prom dress to DonateMyDress.org. DonateMyDress collects and distributes special occasion dresses to girls in need. The goal of the organization is to help girls find the dress of their dreams. Taylor wanted to give another girl a special experience by wearing a beautiful dress on her prom night. Taylor's dress sold for $1,200 in the organization's first celebrity dress charity auction. To learn more about the Donate My Dress Organization, visit **donatemydress.org**.

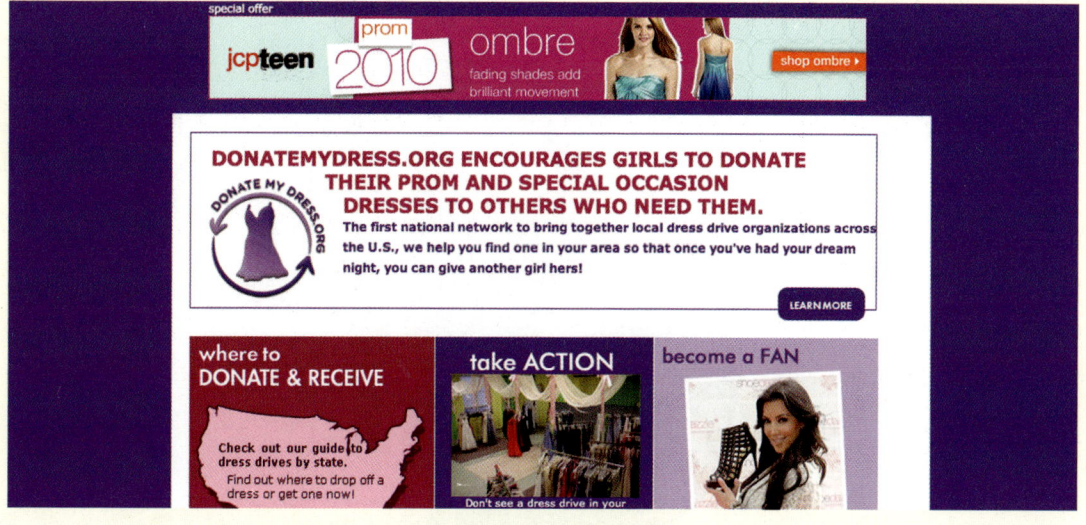

Remarkable People 19

Write a Biography

A person's life story can be the subject of a book. This kind of book is called a biography. Biographies describe the lives of remarkable people, such as those who have achieved great success or have done important things to help others. These people may be alive today, or they may have lived many years ago. Reading a biography can help you learn more about a remarkable person.

At school, you might be asked to write a biography. First, decide whom you want to write about. You can choose a musician, such as Taylor Swift, or any other person you find interesting. Then, find out if your library has any books about this person.

Learn as much as you can about him or her. Write down the key events in the person's life. What was this person's childhood like? What has he or she accomplished? What are his or her goals? What makes this person special or unusual?

A concept web is a useful research tool. Read the questions in the following concept web. Answer the questions in your notebook. Your answers will help you write your biography.

Taylor Swift

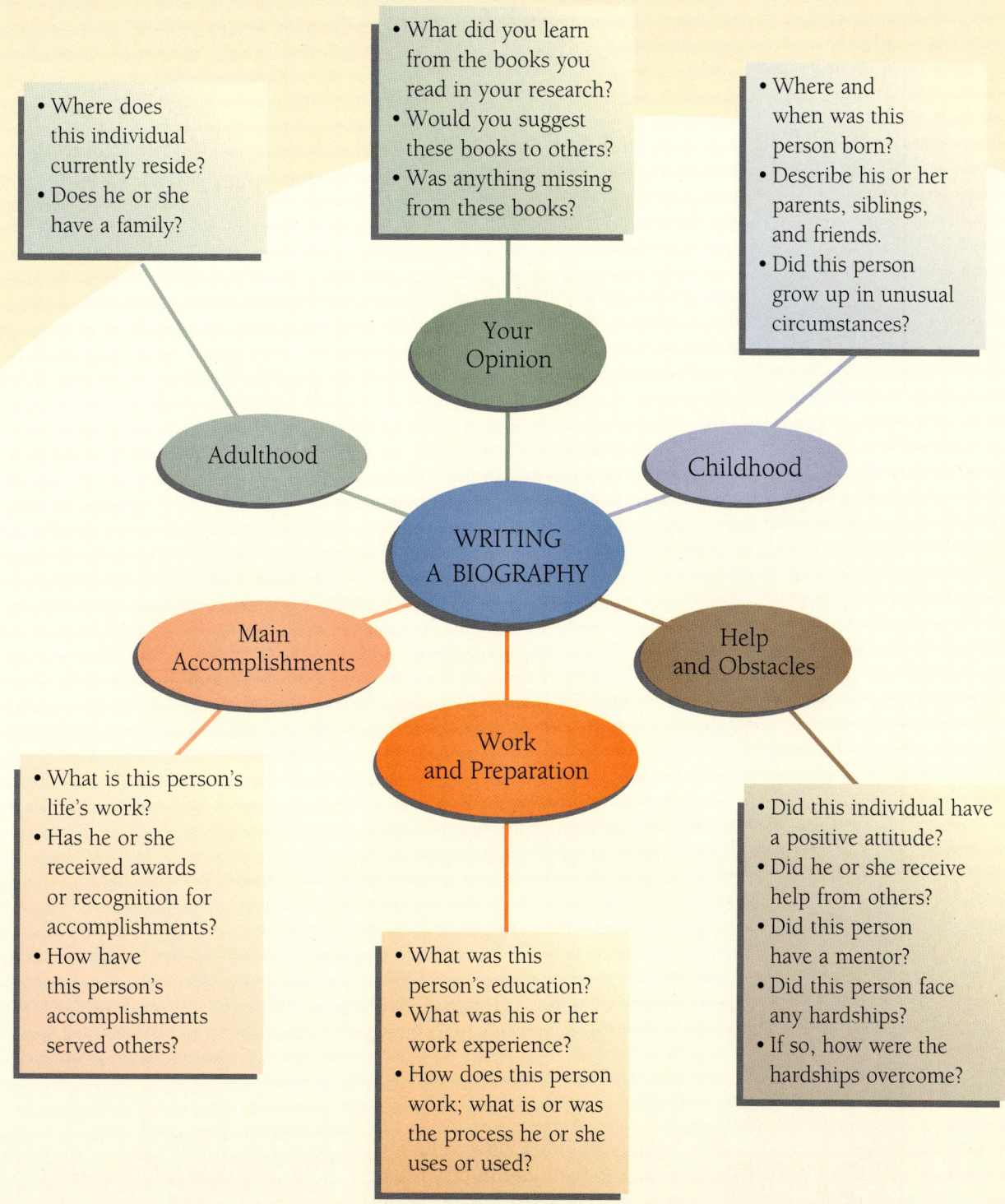

Timeline

YEAR	TAYLOR SWIFT	WORLD EVENTS
1989	Taylor is born in Reading, Pennsylvania.	Michael Jackson receives the Soul Train Heritage Award for his career achievements.
2003	Taylor signs with RCA Records. She is only 13 years of age. She asks to be released from her contract the next year.	Avril Lavigne becomes the second artist in history to have three number one songs from a debut album on the Billboard charts.
2006	Taylor's breakout single "Tim McGraw" peaks at number six on the Billboard Hot Country Songs.	The one-billionth song is downloaded on iTunes.
2006	Taylor's self-titled debut album is released.	Kelly Clarkson is the first American Idol contestant ever to win a Grammy.
2007	Taylor's song "Our Song" reaches number one on the country charts.	The Dixie Chicks win Album of the Year at the Grammy Awards.
2008	Taylor wins the Young Hollywood Award for Superstar of Tomorrow.	Madonna releases her eleventh studio album.
2009	Taylor becomes the youngest singer to win the Country Music Association's Entertainer of the Year Award.	Britney Spears launches her first world tour in five years.

Words to Know

album: a collection of songs released in one package, such as a CD
amplifier: a type of electronic equipment that makes sounds louder
auditioned: performed to try to get a job in the entertainment industry
Billboard: charts produced by a weekly magazine that rate the popularity of music
chords: the playing of three or more musical notes together
choreography: the creation of specific dance steps
competitively: for the purpose of winning a prize
contract: a written agreement to do something
cover versions: performances of songs that were originally recorded by another artist
debut: a first appearance or presentation
demos: trial recordings of songs or an album that are used to attract interest from record companies, musicians, and other artists
double platinum: sold at least two million copies
headline act: the star performer of a show
nominated: added to a small list of people who will be considered for awards
producers: the people who arrange for a album, movie, or television show to be made
record label: a brand used to market music
sets: theater scenery
singles: songs sent out for radio stations to play
stockbroker: a person who buys and sells stocks

Index

Academy of Country Music 18
Bieber, Justin 13
Big Machine Records 9, 17
Billboard 4, 10, 18, 22
Country Music Association 18
Cyrus, Miley 13
Fearless 4, 10, 15, 18
Gomez, Selena 13
Grammy Awards 9, 10, 14, 22, 23
Jonas, Nick 13
MTV 19
Nashville 8, 9, 10, 15, 16
songwriting 8, 9, 10, 11, 12, 13, 15, 16, 17
Sony/ATV 9, 17
Swift, Andrea 6, 15
Swift, Austin 6, 15
Swift, Scott 6, 15
touring 10, 15, 22
Twain, Shania 15, 18
Wyomissing 6

Remarkable People

Log on to www.av2books.com

AV² by Weigl brings you media enhanced books that support active learning. Go to **www.av2books.com**, and enter the special code inside the front cover of this book. You will gain access to enriched and enhanced content that supplements and complements this book. Content includes video, audio, web links, quizzes, a slide show, and activities.

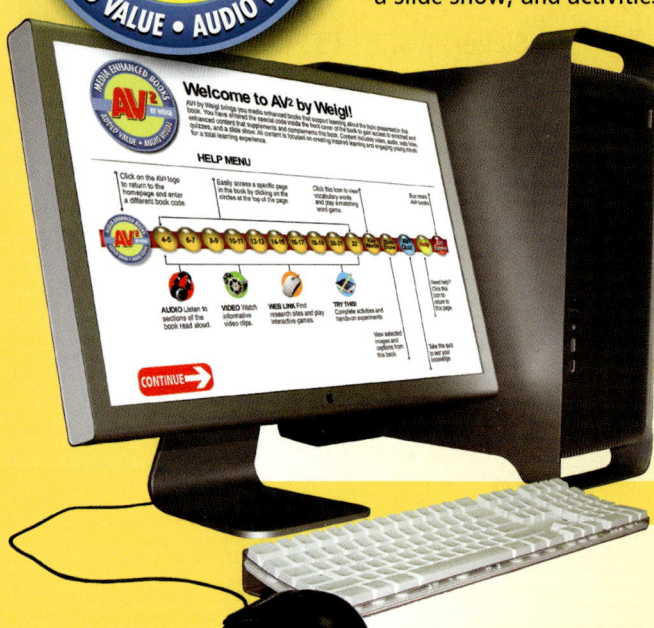

Audio
Listen to sections of the book read aloud.

Video
Watch informative video clips.

Web Link
Find research sites and play interactive games.

Try This!
Complete activities and hands-on experiments.

WHAT'S ONLINE?

 **Try This!** Complete activities and hands-on experiments.	**Web Link** Find research sites and play interactive games.	 **Video** Watch informative video clips.	**EXTRA FEATURES**
Pages 6-7 Complete an activity about your childhood. **Pages 10-11** Try this activity about key events. **Pages 16-17** Complete an activity about overcoming obstacles. **Pages 20-21** Write a biography. **Page 22** Try this timeline activity.	**Pages 8-9** Learn more about Taylor Swift's life. **Pages 14-15** Find out more about the people who influenced Taylor Swift. **Pages 18-19** Learn more about Taylor Swift's achievements. **Pages 20-21** Check out this site about Taylor Swift.	**Pages 4-5** Watch a video about Taylor Swift. **Pages 12-13** Check out a video about Taylor Swift.	**Audio** Hear introductory audio at the top of every page. **Key Words** Study vocabulary, and play a matching word game. **Slide Show** View images and captions, and try a writing activity. **AV² Quiz** Take this quiz to test your knowledge

Due to the dynamic nature of the Internet, some of the URLs and activities provided as part of AV² by Weigl may have changed or ceased to exist. AV² by Weigl accepts no responsibility for any such changes. All media enhanced books are regularly monitored to update addresses and sites in a timely manner. Contact AV² by Weigl at 1-866-649-3445 or av2books@weigl.com with any questions, comments, or feedback.